Jo and Alex
Summer Adventures

By L.S. Winters

Copyright © 2021

L.S. Winters

Cover Illustration by

Mary Tsoukali

ACKNOWLEDGEMENTS

Writing books is harder than I thought but more rewarding than I could ever imagine. Thank you so much to my wonderful husband for being my biggest cheerleader and for encouraging me to keep writing.

I would also like to thank the real-life Ms. Christyna and Dr. Lauren. Thank you for all you do for the communities you serve!

PROLOGUE

Jo and Alex worked hard on Gramma Gladys' farm for two weeks straight. They did chores to earn money so that they could buy new bicycles before summer arrived. They picked delicious apples, collected eggs from the hen house, and helped with the dishes around the farmhouse each and every day.

Alex had a friend named Rosie, who was a chicken, that would wake her up bright and early every morning. During their stay on the farm, Alex decided that she preferred chickens over cats, but that dogs were still her favorite animal. Alex still had not figured out where Rosie disappeared to, and Jo didn't have the heart to tell her.

Jo and Alex went with Gramma Gladys to the farmers market twice. Gramma Gladys was kind enough to organize a table for them. Jo and Alex sold all the apples and eggs that they had collected and worked well together to earn enough money for their very own bicycles. Before going to the farm, they washed cars in their neighborhood in exchange for money. When they had enough money saved up between them, they went together and bought their bicycles!

CHAPTER ONE

Finally, Jo and Alex's dream of having bicycles is a reality. They worked hard for them and they are excited for the adventures ahead!

Jo uses her half of the money to buy a beautiful red bicycle with matching knee pads and a polka dot helmet. Alex uses her half to buy a bright blue bicycle with knee pads to match, plus a white and blue striped helmet.

On the handlebars of their bicycles, they add sparkling silver streamers. Jo and Alex got them so they will have something that matches with each other perfectly, making it very clear to everyone that they are the best of friends.

"Look, they're like short versions of the gymnastics ribbons we play with during recess!" says Jo excitedly. Alex nods happily in agreement.

Jo and Alex have a little bit of money

left over. They decide to save it for a "rainy day," as Jo's father would say. The girls put it safely away in Alex's piggy bank, which stays on the dresser in Alex's room. They figure it is safer than Jo's room, where her little brothers can easily find it. Jo's baby twin brothers have learned to walk now, unsteadily, but still very stealthily when Mom isn't looking. The twins can make it across the room in seconds now! Jo thinks they are going to be more of a handful now when babysitting, so she is not as excited as her mom is about them walking.

On Friday after school, Jo and Alex decide it's time to learn to ride their new bicycles. They wake up early Saturday morning, and instead of reading on Jo's front porch like usual, they put their helmets on and head outside to practice some more. The girls strap on their knee pads and try to ride. They're slowly getting better!

They decide to have a competition to see who can learn to ride a bicycle first. Every time the girls get good momentum on their bicycles, a car comes and they have to stop for safety.

More often than not, the girls get distracted by birds and squirrels while riding. It is very funny, but also not so funny at the same time. At one point, Jo rides her bicycle into a trash bin while trying to avoid a squirrel crossing the road. They didn't realize how many things they had to look for when riding bicycles! Roads and bike trails are all surprisingly full of obstacles to avoid.

Jo and Alex's parents are very proud of how hard they are trying. Every day, the girls come back home beaming with smiles and stories of how fun it has been learning to ride. They are determined to master the bicycles very soon!

On Sunday, Alex is the first to wake up. This is very unusual; Alex is normally a sleepyhead. She is so excited that she wakes Jo up the same way Rosie the chicken used to wake her up when they visited Gramma Gladys' Farm. Alex sometimes still wonders where Rosie disappeared to.

Alex quickly jumps on Jo's bed, giving Jo a big fright!

"Come on, sleepyhead!" laughs Alex. "It's time to conquer our bicycles once and for all!"

Jo first grimaces because she was awakened so suddenly and loudly, but soon realizes it was her best friend who did it. She smiles when she sees the happiness on Alex's face. Jo is still nervous about riding her bike, though. Alex's courage and cheering make it fun, however, when Jo tries to steer and pedal straight.

"Who are you, Rosie the chicken or something?" teases Jo, as she squirms her feet towards Alex to push her off the bed.

"The sun woke me up, lazybones," responds Alex dramatically. "Now get up, or I promise I will eat all the bacon your mom made us for breakfast! Catch me if you can!" Alex says as she hops off the bed before Jo can push her off, and then she runs down the stairs giggling.

"Arrrggg!" is the response Alex hears from the bedroom when she makes it to the top of the stairs. Once Alex gets to the kitchen, she steals a piece of bacon from Jo's plate when Jo's mom isn't looking.

Bacon is Alex's favorite food in the whole wide world; it tastes so delicious! She puts bacon on sandwiches, in salads, but the best is when it is with a hot, yummy breakfast. It makes her tummy grumble when she smells it. Alex thinks to herself that it will be okay to steal one piece off of Jo's plate. Besides, Jo doesn't like it as much as Alex does.

A few moments later, Jo arrives in the kitchen for breakfast. Alex knows today will be the day they learn to ride their bicycles properly. Alex is nervous, too, but more determined now than ever. The girls venture out after breakfast with their helmets and knee pads in tow.

On that same Sunday afternoon, Jo's

parents decide to barbecue in the backyard. They bring out blankets, chairs, and the makings of a delicious family lunch. While the food is cooking on the grill, the twins stumble happily across the lawn. At any moment it seems as though they will fall on their faces, but somehow gravity, or maybe determination, keeps them up! Jo really wants to see the annoying little monsters fall on their faces. The adults are all clapping excitedly, though. Jo and Alex roll their eyes; they don't understand why they are so excited about it. Everyone has to walk eventually, right? Jo's father walks over to help the girls with their bicycles.

"I saw those eyes rolling, little girls," says Jo's father. "We cheered just as much for you when you first took your steps. It's called motivation!"

"Nuh-uh!" responds Jo dramatically, even though she can't remember it. "We were just enjoying how much snot those glazed donut monsters are putting all over Mom's clothes," teases Jo.

Jo's father laughs and hugs her. "Shh...

Don't let your mom hear you call them that. How about I help you master these contraptions, young ladies? Show me how far you've gotten," he says as he points towards the bicycles.

"Yes, please!" the girls chime together.

The girls ride up and down the sidewalk while Jo's father watches. The girls beam proudly when all of their parents clap for them, especially when they turn without falling off and steer back to the barbecue.

"Well done, girls!" says Jo's father proudly. "Looks like your seats could use a bit of adjusting, though. May I?"

Jo and Alex are very excited.

"Yes, please!" They wheel the bicycles to the garage. Jo's father has a wall full of tools. Alex is intrigued by all the different shapes and sizes! She notices that each tool has a place on the wall, outlined and labeled. Jo's father shows them how to find the correct tool to adjust the height of their seats. The girls do it themselves under his careful supervision. Alex really likes learning about tools and fixing things herself!

They head back out and Jo soon realizes the key to riding bicycles.

"C'mon, Alex, the trick is to speed up and to put your foot down quickly when you want to stop," explains Jo to her friend.

"You look like a duck," says Alex and crosses her arms in defiance. Alex is scared she will fall in front of their families, and she doesn't want them to laugh at her.

Alex has always admired how brave Jo is. Right now, though, Jo looks like she might hurt her leg when she stops. The pedal keeps spinning, but the wheels stop. Alex isn't so sure about this, but she wants to be bravet too. She squares her shoulders, flicks her streamers for reassurance, and gives it a go.

"Good job, Alex!" yells Jo from behind her.

Alex pedals faster. She presses the brake softly and sticks out her foot, then remembers to breathe. Alex thanks her lucky stars she didn't fall over this time in front of both their families. Now THAT would have been embarrassing!

"That was terrifying," says a smiling Alex. She turns her bicycle around. "Let me try again. Surely there is a way to be graceful on bicycles. Practice makes perfect!"

Alex and Jo are soon riding the bicycles in circles, up and down the street, laughing all the way! Jo feels free. Alex's dark curly hair has come undone in the wind and is flapping away like a flag. They race each other down the road, then back again.

"If this is freedom, why didn't we try this sooner?!" asks Alex.

"Because bicycles are expensive, silly," responds Jo cleverly.

Since Alex's hair has come undone while riding their bicycles, her mom calls her over so she can brush her hair and make it neat again. Alex can tell her mom is mad while brushing her hair, but she doesn't understand why. It's her hair being pulled by a hurtful brush, after all. Her mom is mumbling under her breath about hair, darn bicycles, and Monday school mornings. Alex wants this to end. She doesn't like having her hair brushed; it takes so long to get the knots out.

"Honey, have you decided if you are going to take the teaching job?" Alex's mom asks her dad.

"No, I haven't yet. It's in the sports department. It will mean I'll have to coach the football team as well," responds her father as he stirs a pot of something that smells yummy.

"Well, it's a great opportunity. Plus, you get to wear a whistle." teases Alex's mom.

"Yes, a shiny silver one which I would use to annoy the kids," her father responds with a smile.

Mom laughs happily. The brush doesn't hurt as much on Alex's head now.

"You always get a whistle when you wear shorts, honey," says Mom, and winks at him.

They both laugh. Alex doesn't understand why. Alex thinks to herself, *This must be one of their 'inside' jokes.* She is just happy Mom isn't brushing her hair so hard anymore.

CHAPTER TWO

Jo and Alex ride their bicycles to the beach. The beach is so close to their home that on some nights, when it is stormy, Jo can hear the waves crashing as she tries to sleep. There is a safe bicycle path that their moms make them promise to stay on the entire way to the beach and back.

Jo wears her matching red knee pads and helmet. Alex also wants to match her bicycle, so she decides to wear her favorite blue top that goes with her helmet and knee pads.

Finally, they get to go on an adventure! It doesn't take the girls long to smell the saltiness in the air and hear the seagulls calling for food. They round the last bend and find a bicycle rack by the boardwalk entrance. Jo and Alex lock their bicycles and race down the boardwalk to the beach. Soon the girls find themselves faced with a blue ocean stretching to the horizon as far as their eyes can see.

Jo and Alex take off their socks and

shoes. When they reach the last step where the boardwalk meets the golden warm sand, they stop. The girls hold hands, jump down, and squirm their feet into the silky sand, giggling happily together.

The beach is their happy place. Jo and Alex love it as much as they love reading books together. They go for a walk down the beach, looking at the pretty shells that have washed up from the ocean. It's still early in the morning, so there aren't many other people around. Jo and Alex find little tracks on the sand. They follow them up into the dunes, only to be stopped by tape and wire around sections of the dunes where the tracks are coming from.

"Hey, you there! You two shouldn't be here," grumbles a loud voice. The girls squeal with fright and grab each other in fear.

Turning slowly, they find themselves face to face with a marine police officer. She has an official-looking clipboard with sunglasses and a hat on. She doesn't seem very happy.

"Sorry, Miss Marine Police Officer," squeaks Jo.

"We were just following the tracks. What are they from?" asks Alex excitedly, impervious to the angry police officer. Alex really wants to know what made the tiny tracks, and the marine police lady looks like the person who would know.

"Ah, those are from the turtle hatchlings. Now go away before you disturb the others," explains the officer, noting something on her clipboard.

Alex and Jo look at each other, shocked. "What do you mean, the others?" pipes up Jo.

"Are you blind? The other baby turtles. Can't you see this area is cordoned off? Look at the sign!"

Clear as day, on the other side of the cordoned off tape is a sign saying, "Do Not Disturb. Sea Turtle Nesting Area." The girls had not seen the sign at all; they were too busy following the little tracks.

"Sorry, Miss Officer, we didn't see the sign until now. We were just curious," says Jo quietly. Jo and Alex turn to go back down the sand dune. The girls are disappointed that they won't be able to see baby turtles. The little tracks are cute, though; they make a runway from the dune to the ocean.

"Okay, fine. I'm sorry I was a bit rude. You can come and look at the others that are hatching. But promise not to touch?" asks the officer seriously.

"Yes, Miss Officer!"

Jo and Alex walk to the marked off area.

"Where are the baby turtles now?" asks Alex. The cordoned off area looks like someone took a pitchfork to it. There are bits of shells similar to eggshells scattered everywhere, but there is no movement to be seen.

responds Alex with a shrug.

Jo laughs and hugs her.

"You are always so ready for action, Alex! Except in the mornings when you have to wake up,'' teases Jo. "I have a secret I want to tell you," Jo continues shyly. "Pinky swear it will stay between us, though!"

"Of course. What is it?" asks Alex.

"I love the ocean," explains Jo. "I also love coming to the beach and playing in the sand. I think it's cool how turtles can swim all over the world, but one thing I haven't learned to do yet is swim."

"Okay. That's not a secret, though, silly billy!" says Alex. Alex can see her friend is extremely uncomfortable now. Jo's head is down, her shoulders are sad-looking, and she won't look at her. Alex hugs her. "I can teach you how to swim! I love the water! I still have my floaties, and we can find a book about it, too."

"Your floaties?" asks Jo, confused.

"Yes, my floaties. They are plastic wings you put on your arms and they help you stay afloat," explains Alex patiently. "My mom got them for me when I learned to swim at our old house. They'll fit you, too, and they're even your favorite color, red!"

Back at Alex's house, Alex is paddling across the pool, her head above the water, and Jo is standing on the side of the pool looking at her like she's grown a third head. Alex loves the water; she used to swim in competitions at her old school.

"See, all you do is move your legs like this and scoop your arms!" explains Alex.

Jo feels uncomfortable. She is standing on the side of the pool in her swimsuit with the red inflatable floaties on.

"I don't know if I can do this…" says Jo quietly.

"Of course you can," Alex replies, encouraging her.

"What if these floaties fall off, or what if I am not strong enough to keep my head up?" asks Jo.

"That's why I'm here! We will stay in the shallow end, going from one shallow side to the other. You will be able to stand up anytime you want. I also have pool noodles, look!" Alex lifts the two noodles in her hands. "Grab on to these. If a floatie comes off, you'll stay floating on the surface." Alex grabs the floats. She tucks the pool noodles under her arms and kicks across the shallow side to show Jo how easy it is.

The inflatable floaties on her arms are so tight they squeeze Jo's arms. Alex said that's how they're supposed to fit. Jo walks in slowly and sighs.

They spend all afternoon in the pool. Together they conquer Jo's fear of swimming. Soon she is swimming like a mermaid from one end to the other.

Jo and Alex are very excited to go swimming in the ocean together now. Maybe they will see the baby turtles the tracks belonged to!

CHAPTER THREE

The library is Jo and Alex's destination of choice for their next adventure.

Jo has a library card and thinks it will be a good idea to get Alex one, too, even though Alex has over a hundred books at home.

"The library has THOUSANDS of books," explains Jo.

"Thousands?" asks Alex. "In our old town, we had a library, too. I would go there with Chantel after school while my parents were at work. Mom said it was a safe place to wait for them and learn about new adventures. That's when I learned that I love reading."

Alex is very excited to go to the library with Jo. Jo is nervous and excited to show Alex one of her favorite places.

Alex wonders if she is the only one who has ever thought that a book smells nice. *Old books are smelly but have character*, she thinks to herself. *They have bookmarked ears,*

*and maybe even stains or notes from other
people long ago.*

If Alex is being honest with herself, she
thinks about where books come from just as
much as the stories themselves.

Jo and Alex get permission from their
parents before making the journey. Jo knows
the route very well, and it's one of her favorite
places to go. The girls agree to go on Friday
after school, but they have to be home before
dinner time.

"C'mon, Jo! You know I have no
patience!" says Alex on Friday after the school
bell rings. Alex wants to visit the library now;
school felt like it took forever to be over today!

Jo laughs. "Race you to our bicycles,
you turtle!"

Alex looks at Jo running down the
hallway, thinking to herself, *Don't turtles
belong in the ocean or the sea? Does Jo mean
tortoise, then?*

Then Alex remembers she should be running, too. She shrugs and chases after her best friend.

The girls park their bikes in the bicycle stand in front of the library. They have the whole afternoon to spend getting lost in books!

In front of them are massive wooden doors. Alex thinks that this set of doors could be in one of the adventure books she reads. It has faces, flowers, and mountains carved into the wood. To Alex, the doors look like they belong to a wizard's house!

Jo is talking again, so Alex forces herself to pay attention.

"So we need to leave here by 5 p.m. to be home by dinnertime. How does that sound?" Jo asks.

Alex agrees with a nod of her head while her eyes are still transfixed to the door. She is trying very hard to pay attention to Jo, but the door is too beautiful!

Alex looks at Jo. "Can we go in now, pleeeeease?"

Jo laughs.

"Yes, welcome to the library!" responds Jo dramatically. She pulls the door open, raising her arms up and open in triumph.

"Shhh!" comes a sound from behind a desk. It is clearly directed at the girls. An old lady is standing there, thin, with gray hair. Alex thinks that she looks mean. Gramma Gladys has gray hair, too, but she smiles more.

To Alex, this lady looks like she hasn't smiled in a long time.

How can a librarian not be happy with so many adventures around them? wonders Alex.

"Sorry, Ms. Roberts," says a blushing Jo, clapping her hand to her mouth. Jo then leans towards Alex, whispering, "That's Ms. Roberts. She's the mean one. Stay away from her."

Jo grabs Alex's hand and they walk

over to the lockers. The girls store their bicycle keys, helmets, and knee pads.

"This place smells like adventure, Jo," says Alex excitedly. "Despite the grumpy Roberts lady!"

"I think so, too!" whispers Jo. "I want you to meet someone. Her name is Ms. Christyna. She is much happier than Ms. Roberts. She's always at the library. I think she lives here because you can always find her somewhere in the library packing the returned books away neatly. She has the prettiest dresses! Also, if you have a question or an adventure you'd like to read about, she always has the best answers. She will tell you the best books to read, but you have to keep quiet. Okay? 'Most people come here to go on their own adventures,' Ms. Christyna always says."

"I *have* been in a library before, remember? But it's a deal. C'mon, let's go find her then!" responds Alex, dragging her friend forward.

Alex soon realizes that she has no idea where she is going. She starts walking next to

Jo instead. The girls venture deeper into the library. This library is the biggest one Alex has ever seen!

Jo and Alex are as excited as they were when they visited the circus. Alex can't believe how high the shelves are. She strains her neck back to try to see the top of the shelves. The racks of books stand tall and in line as far as the eye can see in the big room. There is a second level of the building with even more books! It runs to the outer edge of the building. Alex is shocked at how many books there are here.

"Jo, is that you?" says the prettiest voice Alex has ever heard.

Both girls turned around.

There stands Ms. Christyna. Alex knows it has to be her. Jo squeals quietly in delight.

Ms. Christyna wears a knee-length blue dress with white stars. Her happy smiling face is tilted inquiringly towards them.

Jo was right, thinks Alex. *Ms. Christyna is beautiful!*

"Ms. Christyna!" says Jo with a smile, running to her and giving her a big hug.

"I'm sorry it's been so long since my last visit," says Jo. "I was learning to ride my new bicycle with Alex!"

"That's wonderful news, Jo!" responds Ms. Christyna, cupping her cheeks. "You don't look too bruised up, so I'm guessing you did fabulously well as always?"

Jo smiles from ear to ear.

Alex is staring at her feet shyly. She finds that playing with the hem of her shirt is all of sudden very interesting. Ms. Christyna is so excited to see Jo that Alex feels like a third wheel.

Jo looks at her best friend. She is playing with her shirt like she does when Miles Porter is nearby. She doesn't understand why Alex is being so quiet.

"Oh, yes! There is someone I want you

to meet," says Jo. "This is Alex, my best friend in the whole world! She is kind of new in town and loves books like we do, Ms. Christyna! How great is that?"

"Pleased to meet you, Miss Alex," says Ms. Christyna politely, holding out her hand. "Welcome to the library."

"Thank you, Ms. Christyna. It's lovely to meet you, too," responds Alex.

There is an awkward silence. Alex is not sure what to say next. She wants to run behind one of the book racks and look at all the books.

"Can we please get Alex a library card?" asks Jo.

"Of course. Let's go to the front desk. Tell me, what adventures have you two been having on your bicycles?" asks Ms. Christyna.

"We went to the beach and saw baby turtle tracks. Then Jo and I went swimming; she is now comfortable in the pool, thanks to my floaties and pool noodles! The library is our second adventure now on our bicycles. We want to learn more about the turtles we found on the beach," responds Alex confidently. They all make their way back to the front desk.

"And did you know that only one in a thousand make it to being an adult?" interjects Jo.

"Why, no, I didn't," responds Ms. Christyna. "That's incredible!" She pulls out a form for Alex. "Here you go, Miss Alex; this is the form for your very own card. You will need to fill this out with your parents. Then your parents must sign here, and you over here." She points to two lines at the bottom of the page. "After that, you can check out a book!"

"Thank you, Ms. Christyna. Do you mind if we go look for some books about turtles and I'll give the form to my parents later?" asks Alex, looking down at the form. "I don't want to go home just yet. It smells like adventure in here."

Ms. Christyna laughs warmly at Alex's enthusiasm.

"Of course, Jo knows where the best adventures are. Turtles are in Section D, Shelf 6 in the non-fiction area," smiles Ms. Christyna. "Why don't you show your best friend your favorite reading spot, Jo?"

"Great idea," says Jo. "We just have to head home at 5 p.m."

"I will be sure to remind you two, then," says Ms. Christyna. "Go on, now!"

"Thank you, Ms. Christyna," chime the girls.

The girls spend the whole afternoon in the fiction corner. Alex loves seeing so many books in one place! Jo has a stack of books she is interested in checking out. She is flipping through each one, reading a few pages then dividing them up into a yes and no pile.

At 5 p.m. Ms. Christyna finds them and reminds them it's time to go home. It's not the first time that Jo thinks to herself how fast time flies when she is reading books. Jo checks out two new books. Alex still has to get her library card form signed by her parents before she can check out any.

"Now remember, I don't want any ketchup stains on those books, Miss Jo!" whispers Ms. Roberts over Ms. Christyna's shoulder at checkout.

"Yes, Ms. Roberts," responds Jo politely. Jo is blushing but her face looks mad.

The girls thank Ms. Christyna and leave.

"Why did you blush and look mad at the same time?" asks Alex.

"Because it was my little brothers who flicked ketchup on me while I was reading in the kitchen last time," explains Jo. She stomps her foot in frustration. "Ms. Roberts thinks it was me, that I did it on purpose. She won't even listen to what REALLY happened," finishes Jo dramatically, clipping on her helmet and then unlocking their bicycles.

"It's okay. You know the truth,"

explains Alex. "Some people don't like listening, that's all."

"I know the truth, and so does Ms. Christyna," clarifies Jo. "She always listens. Let's go. We're going to be late for dinner if we don't leave now!"

Alex rides her bicycle straight across the last street on their way home from the library.

In her haste, she misses the ramp by a tire's width and instead hits the curb. Immediately, the bicycle stops dead in its tracks. Jo watches helplessly as Alex is flung clean over the handlebars towards the hard pavement. Unfortunately, Alex's face plants with all that forward speed, splat! Right on the concrete.

Jo is shocked! She screams, scrambling off her bike, and rushes over to shake her friend's shoulders to make sure she is okay.

"Are you all right, Alex? Wake up, Alex!" says a very worried Jo. Alex looks like a limp doll.

"Arrrg, ouch," responds Alex, finally moving. "That really hurt!" she continues, bringing her hand up to her face.

Alex's helmet is askew, and while it did protect her precious, intelligent brain, it did not cover her beautiful face. Alex has scratch marks on the right side of her face, and a gross metallic taste in her mouth that she wants to spit out.

She spits out blood and a piece of a tooth with wide, shocked eyes. Jo and Alex both stare at the tiny little bit of her tooth. Clearly it came out of Alex's mouth because she fell so hard on her face.

Alex breaks the silence first.

"Well, that stinks," she grumbles. Tears are starting to well up. Her vision is blurry. She doesn't want to cry in the street like this, but her face really hurts now.

Jo squares her shoulders, whips out her cell phone, and declares "I'll call my mom! It will be okay."

Jo dials the one person in the world who will always come to her rescue, confident that her mom will know what to do.

CHAPTER FOUR

Jo's mom finds them sitting on the sidewalk. Jo has her arm around a teary-eyed Alex. She thinks Alex's face looks really sore; it's starting to swell where Alex fell on it.

Mom tells them to get in the car while she quickly throws both of their bicycles in the back of the van. Jo's mom calls Alex's mom before starting the car. Alex's mom says she is going to meet them at the dentist's office.

Jo holds Alex's hand really tight all the way to the dentist.

Jo is very proud of how brave and fearless Alex is being. Alex has stopped crying now. She reminds Jo of the heroes in stories she loves to read: courage, despite the danger looming.

Jo does not like dentists and dentists do not like her. It is a proven fact in Jo's mind especially after the last time Jo saw one. The dentist hurt her, so she bit his finger. Jo thinks that Mom will not be very happy if she tells that story to Alex right now, though.

Maybe after Alex is finished at the dentist? It's a funny story, after all, thinks a distracted Jo. Alex's broken front tooth looks very painful. Jo does not want to scare her courage away. She hopes that her mom won't be too mad at them for getting hurt.

Alex still doesn't feel the pain that should be in her face.

She thinks, *Is this what the heroes in my book call adrenaline, maybe?*

Alex knows she should be sore, but she isn't. She cried on the pavement out of fright more than anything. Jo's mom is looking at Alex with a worried face as she speeds to the dentist's office. The bleeding in Alex's mouth tastes like it has stopped, though. Alex is rolling the piece of her front tooth around in her hand.

Alex wonders, *How can something so tiny cause so much worry?*

Alex's mom meets them at the dentist's office. Alex notices that her mom looks really worried, so she confidently runs up to her and hugs her.

"It's okay, Mom. My face doesn't hurt." She looks up at her mom. The concern in her face worries Alex, but she hurriedly continues talking to try to calm her fears. "Jo helped me up quickly. She's a great friend. My bicycle isn't broken, and I didn't mean to fall, I swear it!"

"Oh, Alex! I don't care about the bicycle. I'm worried about you, my brave little girl!" responds Mom as she hugs Alex to her chest tighter. "I'm just glad you are still standing. That call nearly gave me a heart attack. Thank you for bringing her," she says to Jo's mom. "Let's get you in to the dentist."

Alex is relieved that her mom is not mad. That's a win already! She hopes her mom will stop worrying. Jo's mom and Jo sit in the waiting room while they walk further in.

"Hello. I am your dentist today. What can I help you with?" says a gray-haired man when Alex enters the room with her mom. The doctor is wearing a long white coat, with brown glasses on his nose and a friendly smile plastered on his face.

The doctor motions to the chair in the middle of the bright room. On either side of the seat are two tables that swing back and forth on white arms when the doctor pushes them open for her. Alex stands near a long blue chair that is double her length. The long chair looks like it can lie all the way down. On the left side of the chair is a cup and a drain, and the other side has a swinging table with rows of shiny silver tools, little mirrors, picks, jars lined up, and four little drill handles hanging from it.

Alex is very intrigued by all the tools. She knows they are drills from previous visits to the dentist in her old town even though they look different from the ones her father showed her how to use when they made a birdhouse last summer.

These are very tiny fancy-looking drills,

thinks Alex.

The most facinating thing of all is the big white light peeking out of the top of this entire contraption. No, not the one from the ceiling in the room. This white light is on a big arm and sits directly over the chair. It has a brighter white light, with a handle on it to steer it around. Alex is amazed by it. The shape of the light reminds her of the robot from the movie *Wall-E*.

"Hi, I'm Alex," she says to the dentist.

"Hi, Alex. I am Dr. Porter," he replies as he holds out his hand for a handshake.

Alex is very impressed with his manners. *Dad would like him,* she thinks.

"Let's have a quick look-see. What happened here?" he asks as he walks closer towards Alex. "Please, lie down here." He pats the long blue seat. "I am going to put this bib around your neck. Then can I have a look at your chompers, please, Miss Alex?"

Alex laughs. Her face still doesn't hurt yet. Chompers. She hasn't heard anyone say that since they stayed with her grandparents. "Go brush your chompers before bed," Nana would say every night.

Alex is feeling more comfortable. She looks at her mom. Her mom gives her an encouraging nod, the same one she does when everything is okay. Mom only wants Alex to sit and listen. Alex does not want to open her mouth but does for the doctor. She is embarrassed. She thinks her smile must be hideous and is sure it's full of blood.

"Okay, so first we need to clean your mouth and stop the bleeding," says Dr. Porter. He hands her a cup of water. "This is rinse is going to sting, like a pin pricking on the bleeding parts, but it will help a lot to clean out the wounds. Gargle it, count to fifteen, then spit it all out in the drain for me."

Alex is trying very hard to be brave. She wants to trust the kind doctor in front of her. For some reason, his name sounds familiar. Alex can't remember where she has heard it before. She takes the water, gargles it, and then spits it in the drain. It tastes like the ocean when she and Jo go to the beach together. *That's a happy thought,* thinks Alex.

"That wasn't so bad," she says bravely.

"Good job, Miss Alex," he says. "Now open wide one more time, please."

Alex does what the dentist asks, opening her mouth wide after he puts the bib around her neck. So wide that he can probably see the bacon and eggs she had for breakfast!

Alex thinks, *Maybe I fell because I stole that piece of extra bacon when Jo wasn't looking?* She swears to herself that she won't do that again. Jo can have all the bacon in the world from now on!

"Hmm," he says, pulling the bright white light right over Alex's head. Dr. Porter now has gloves on and a thing in his hand--a tiny round mirror. "Aaaah, I see the little nugget."

Dr. Porter stands up and walks to his

computer where he types in some notes.

Alex closes her mouth and looks around the room. The white *Wall-E* light is right above her head, and it blinds her eyes every time she looks up from the chair.

The room smells funny. Clean, though, very clean. The same smell of the bathroom, like when Mom has been cleaning all Saturday morning.

He walks back a second time and takes one of his tools and prods at her teeth. "Just a little more please, Miss Alex. Nearly done."

Alex nods to his words and opens her mouth wider. She feels her mom's hand grab hers softly and squeeze. Alex finds this very reassuring. Mom is the bravest mom in the whole world. She won't let the dentist hurt Alex.

Dr. Porter turns to Mom and asks for the little tooth that fell out of Alex's mouth. Mom hands it to him.

"Well, have a look here," says Dr. Porter. "You are in luck! All your teeth look great. No crack other than the tooth that broke. It's a baby tooth. One of your last two, actually. You are a very lucky young lady. Yes, it is your front tooth, but the other half of it is already loose from your fall." He pats Alex's shoulder reassuringly. "I can take the sharp edges away from the tooth, and in a day or two it should fall out on its own, since you fell so well. Or I can pull it out for you now if you'd like?"

"Thank you, doctor. What do you think, Alex? I think having it pulled would be better," says Mom. She seems very relieved at the good news.

"Okay, Mom, but will it hurt? And how much longer till I am fixed, Dr. Porter?" asks Alex.

"You aren't broken," laughs Dr. Porter. He has the brightest blue eyes Alex has ever seen. "Your teeth are still changing, that's all. To pull it out it will take another fifteen minutes or so. I am going to apply some anesthetic, Alex. Then I have to inject you with some more to help with pain. She isn't allergic to anything, is she?"

"No, she will be fine," says Alex's mom. She squeezes her hand again. "She is my little warrior."

Alex's fear disappears with the love in her mom's eyes. Even though the room smells funny, the chair she is lying on is uncomfortable, and Dr. Porter said inject which means he is going to use a needle, she knows everything is going to be okay. Alex's mom is here, and Jo is waiting outside.
The kind Dr. Porter holds up a piece of white cotton with pink goo on it. "This is anesthetic. It is going to taste yummy, but please don't lick it. We need to leave it on your gums. It will help me to work quicker on your teeth by making them numb so that I won't hurt you."

Alex nods. She sits patiently as the doctor takes the goo and places it inside her top lip, right above the broken tooth.

"Now, how do you feel about needles,

excitedly.

"Great!" responds Jo. "So, what about Kimberly and Jenny? Also Tara from the farmers market? Gramma Gladys knows her, so I can call for her number. Then Miles and Ariana, do you think they will come?"

"Of course they will come, silly," says Alex confidently. "We are nice to them. Why wouldn't they?"

"That's true," admits Jo. Alex is always so nice to everyone. Jo likes that about her best friend.

After finishing the list, Jo and Alex get help from Alex's mom with the invites. The invites are teal blue, with sea stars and snorkel faces on it. To the girls, they look like the coolest birthday invitations they have ever seen!

Jo and Alex receive news that everyone they invited to their joint birthday party is coming, even Grampa Mark and Gramma Gladys.

Mr. Sam says he has to stay on the farm, though. "Someone has to watch the farm while Gramps is away," says Mr. Sam. "Besides, Bessie doesn't like sand in her fur. Thank you for thinking of me, though, my little giggle pots. Come visit us soon, yah hear!"

It's August 1st, Jo and Alex's birthday. You would think that they are both woken up by their families with presents and balloons, but only one of them is.

Alex is woken up by her mom and dad singing "Happy Birthday" with a present. Cleary, the beautifully wrapped gift is in the shape of a book. Alex is very happy. She even has pancakes and bacon for breakfast. Her older sister Chantel wakes up with the rest of the family to join them when the smell of bacon wafts upstairs. Alex is very excited to have a beach party with all their friends today. She gets a new swimsuit from her sister as a birthday present, blue with white stars on it.

Jo is not awakened by her parents. Instead of waking up to presents and happy faces like Alex is, Jo is awakened by her brothers. The twins had gotten into the habit of climbing out of their beds now. They had learned to walk over the past few months. Mom is no longer impressed with how fast they are moving.

On her birthday, Jo opens her eyes to her two brothers standing next to her bed. The first thing Jo notices is how snotty their noses are.

Jo likes to think of them as "glazed donut monsters." Her father thinks the nickname is funny because their snot always runs down their faces and over their top lip. Mom, on the other hand, is not happy with the nickname. So it's her father and Jo's inside joke when Mom isn't around.

The second thing Jo notices is that one of them is poking her in the cheek, while the other is giggling with his hands over his mouth. His clothes are oddly wet, even his hair.

Lastly, she hears water. Lots of water running, like the sound of a waterfall coming from the bathroom. A feeling of dread settles in

Jo's tummy.

The twins run out of her bedroom giggling.

"Mooooootheeer!" shouts Jo when her sleepy brain finally registers what's happening. Pulling off her covers, Jo runs to the bathroom.

All the faucets are on! The shower is a walk-in shower, and it's spewing water at full force. In front of the sinks are the twins' little steps they use when they brush their teeth. Both faucets are on there as well. She hears her mom get out of bed and run past the bathroom with only a glance, then straight downstairs. The kitchen sink is also running. Today is going to be a long day.

Alex runs out to meet her best friend in the whole world on their birthday.

After breakfast, the girls have plans to pack the two cars with all the beach stuff they need for their party. They are finally double digits, the big ten. Alex feels older than yesterday.

Alex finds Jo lying on the grass with a book over her face, fast asleep.

"Wakey wakey, sleepyhead," says Alex as she drops Jo's present on her tummy, waking her up.

"Not again... Oh, it's you, Alex. I woke up to dire things this morning," says Jo tiredly. She pulls out Alex's present. Finally, Jo is feeling excited about it being her birthday. Alex's happiness is contagious. "Here you go, you first. Happy birthday, Alex!"

Jo framed a photo of them. The frame has little turtles around the edges and on the top is the words "Best Friends Forever." The picture is the one Jo's mom took when they left the dentist. The girls are smiling happily in the picture, with their arms draped around each other. You can also clearly see Alex is missing her front tooth. It was the scariest and funniest day ever.

"Thank you, Jo," says Alex, wrapping her best friend in a big hug. "I love it! It's going to go next to Mr. Piggy on my dresser. Now it's your turn," she says as she hands Jo a square box.

Jo unwraps it quickly. Inside is a book called *Little Women*. It's a beautiful old hardcover that looks like it's been read by many people.

"It's one of my favorite books in the whole wide world," explains Alex. "I hope you like it!"

Jo opens the cover and finds a note from Alex.

To Jo: thanks for being my best friend. I love our adventures together, and I hope you enjoy this adventure as much as I did. Hugs, Alex. P.S. BFF forever xxx

"Thank you so much!" says Jo, beaming with a smile. "It's beautiful!"

CHAPTER SIX

Jo and Alex's birthday party is going to be a blast!

Today is the perfect day for the beach; the sun is out, and the ocean is the prettiest blue color. There are lots of people enjoying the day together.

The girls help their parents set up a beach canopy for some shade. Two long tables are quickly set out. One is for the food and drinks, the other for presents and sunscreen.

The rule is made clear: sunscreen before candy.

All of Jo and Alex's friends arrive for their fun morning on the beach.

"There are my farm buddies!" yells Jackson as he runs down from the parking lot to greet them.

Both Jo and Alex squeal with delight

and tackle their friend for a hug. Jean is not far behind, loaded with towels and hiding beneath a wide-brimmed hat and cool black sunglasses.

"Hello, troublemakers!" she teases happily. "Happy birthday!" She gives them a big kiss on the cheek. Jean hands them the two prettiest little teal boxes with white bows and the words "Tiffany Co." on them.

"Thank you for coming!" says an excited Jo. "But I think you are mistaken. They don't have our names on them. They actually say Tiffany. Who is she? Maybe she is missing her present?"

"No, silly," says Jean with a laugh. "Tiffany is the company that makes it. They are for special girls. Inside are your very own charm bracelets. I put three matching charms on them, one for each of your initials, one that says girl power, and a tiny bicycle. I thought it would be nice to have something to remember our first summer together."

Jo is speechless. It is such a kind and sweet gift!

"It's very thoughtful," says Alex. "I will treasure it forever and ever!"

Alex loves the pretty silver bracelet. It is so beautiful and shiny. Alex is very surprised by how someone who was so mean to them on the farm can now be so nice after a little bit of love and understanding. Maybe Jean and Chantel can resolve their differences as well?

Once the rest of their friends arrive, they start the JOLEX Olympic Games. Jo and Alex came up with games to keep everyone busy and happy at their birthday party. They even made a scoreboard to keep everyone motivated. The grand prize is a bag full of candy.

Jo's team is the red team. Alex's team is the blue team. Their friends pull straws for their colored hat, red or blue. They all then line up for a chocolate and some sunscreen.

The first game is to see who can make

the best sandcastle. Jo's dad says they have twenty minutes to complete it. The judges are going to be the dads, and Gramma Gladys. Gramma Gladys is under the canopy, safely in the shade looking after the food and presents. She is sipping on a large water bottle. Strangely, she is very strict about who can have some of her water. Jo thinks it's not water inside the bottle.

The castle building competition is a lot of fun! The boys dig furiously, building a good foundation. Even Grampa Mark helps Jo's team with hers. The girls look for shells to decorate the outside of the castle, and others start digging moats so that the ocean doesn't wash it way too fast.

Everyone is giggling and racing to make the best sandcastle. Alex loves playing in the sand. Chantel is helping her with their sandcastle. Chantel has an eye for detail.

Soon, the whistle blows and the judging begins. Gramma Gladys declares the blue team the winner! All of a sudden the twins make an appearance. They run giggling straight into the blue team's sandcastle. Everyone yells, "No!" as the twins scramble over it.

The boys giggle and run back to the canopy where Jo's mom is busy taking out the birthday cake.

"Well, I'm glad we got the judging out of the way first," laughs Gramma Gladys.

Next, they all wash off in the ocean. They try their best to clean the sand off their hands, then make their way back to the canopy.

The candles are lit, and everyone starts singing. "Happy Birthday to you! Happy Birthday to you…!"

Jo and Alex beam with joy. This is the best day ever! The cake is in the shape of a turtle with lots of baby turtle cupcakes around it. They blow out their candles together as their friends and family finish singing.

Everyone enjoys a slice of their yummy chocolate cake.

Alex's mom yells, "Race you to the ocean, girls!" and runs down towards the ocean, laughing.

"Wait for me!" yells Jo's mom.

Jo and Alex are shocked, but happy. They run after their moms, laughing and splashing into the ocean.

Alex's mom yells, "It's so much colder than I thought!"

"Dunk your head under," says Alex. "Then you get used to it quicker. Like this!" She ducks under the water and bolts right out after the wave passes, giggling. "See, it's easy!" She turns towards her mom.

Alex's mom isn't there anymore. Jo can't see her at all as she looks around.

All of a sudden Alex feels something on her leg. She yells and turns to run out of the ocean.

"Booo!" her mom says as she jumps

out of the water, giving her the biggest fright. "It's the tickle monster mermaid!" She laughs as Alex runs away in fright. Realizing it's only her mom, she turns back around and runs into her and they both fall down laughing in the shallow water.

Jo is not far away diving under the waves with her mom. Suddenly, Alex hears a scream. It's not the happy, "I'm having fun" type of scream. To Alex, it sounds like someone's hurt. She looks around to see where it came from and spots Jo being carried out the water by her mom. Jo doesn't look very happy. She looks hurt!

At first, Jo thinks jellyfish are pretty. All the books she read about them in the library explained that they are peaceful creatures. So Jo doesn't understand then why such a peaceful creature would hurt her.

Jo's leg stings. It stings worse than the time she was stung by a bee! There are red lumpy lines around her leg where the jellyfish tried to say hello to her while they were playing in the water for her birthday party.

Jo does not like how her leg is swelling up; it is very itchy where it stung her. She's feeling very nauseated now. Her mom looks upset while rushing her towards the car.

Jo tries to tell her mom she is fine. Her mom isn't listening. So Jo sits down in front of the car and refuses to get in.

"I'm FINE!" yells Jo to her mom. Jo has not told her that she is nauseated. She wants to stay at their birthday party on the beach. "I'm sure Alex will pee on me if I ask her, Mom. That's what a book I read said to do!"

"Joanna Elizabeth Powers!" yells Jo's mom back when she puts down the phone. "No one is peeing on you, young lady! You are having an allergic reaction to the jellyfish sting. Now get in the car. I am taking you to the emergency room!"

Jo knows better than to argue with her mom when she uses her full name. It just makes things worse. Jo sadly hops into the car. Tears are running down her face now. This was supposed to be Alex's and her day to celebrate together.

How many best friends can say they have the same birthday? thinks Jo.

When they drive away, Jo waves to Alex, who is standing with her family looking worried. Jo's tummy doesn't feel well at all, as if somehow a volcano is erupting in her belly. Jo wishes with her whole heart that she can stay. Jo's tummy feels like it's crawling up her throat.

"Mom, can I please have a bag?" "What for? We are five minutes away. Hang in there, Jo," responds her mom as she leans over and squeezes Jo's knee in reassurance. Noticing how pale Jo's face is becoming, her mom's face deepens with worry.

Very quietly Jo responds, "A volcano wants to come out. I think I'm going to puke, Mom."

Jo's mom grabs a bag quickly and hands it to Jo. Jo feels terrible now. She throws up into the bag as her mom strokes her hair reassuringly while keeping her eyes on the road. They arrive at the emergency room within a few minutes.

Jo's head hurts and she wants to lie down. Her mom tells her she can't yet, she has to see the doctor first. Jo keeps on puking up her birthday cake into the bag.

What a waste of a yummy cake! It definitely does not taste better the second time, thinks Jo sadly.

Dr. Lauren has the prettiest brown eyes Jo has ever seen. She smiles down at Jo and takes her temperature. Jo feels really tired. She thinks Dr. Lauren looks very happy. She likes Dr. Lauren. Jo watches as she picks out all of the stingers from the jellyfish. It stings a lot!

"You're doing great, Miss Jo," says Dr. Lauren soothingly as she tends to her leg. She then places the hottest cloth Jo has ever felt over her sting.

"It will be okay," explains Dr. Lauren. "This is called a hot compress. It breaks down the proteins from the sting, making them useless a lot quicker. It will help with the itching. Now, do you feel tired, nauseated?"

Jo wants to be brave, but her mom has that face on that means business.

"I want to sleep, but my mom said I have to meet you first. I threw up in the car," responds Jo. "I'm sorry, Mom."

"It's okay, Jo," says Mom sadly, walking over and holding her hand.

"You did very well, Jo. I'm happy to meet you," says Dr. Lauren "You're very young, and this sting is over a big area. Your body is fighting the sting, so that's why you are so tired. Are you feeling better since you threw up?"

Jo nods.

In the end, Dr. Lauren gives Jo a hug

and thanks her for being brave. She finds herself thinking about Miles Porter. She saw him arrive at her and Alex's birthday party but she doesn't know if he saw her get stung by the silly jellyfish or not.

She feels very embarrassed at the thought of Miles Porter seeing her like this. She hopes he will still talk to her at school.

The next day it's another birthday in the family.

Jo and her mom make breakfast for her dad on his birthday. Jo's mom bought him socks and a framed picture of them as a family. Her dad loves silly socks. He must have a hundred pairs.

Jo put special thought into her dad's birthday present this year, using her extra money from the bicycle fund. Jo looked for something funny for her very cool dad. She made the best present in the whole world, in her opinion. She is very excited to see his reaction at breakfast!

Jo's dad was smiling over his presents

as he unwrapped them while having coffee. Finally, he gets to unwrapping Jo's.

"You're going to love it, Dad!" says Jo excitedly.

His eyebrows rise up as he holds up the shirt in front of him and reads the words out loud in a funny voice:

"How much for the angry lawn gnome?"
"Hey, that's my toddler! I call it a glazed donut monster!"

"Joanna!" yells Jo's mom.

Jo and her dad burst into laughter. They laugh so hard their tummies hurt and they cry. Jo is crying not because she is sad; she is crying because of her dad's face, and her mom's reaction is hilarious!

Even though her mom sounds mad, Jo does notice the smile she has when she turns around and walks back to the kitchen. It's funny! Mom just won't admit it because she doesn't like the nickname for Jo's twin brothers.

"My dad loved it!" says Jo as she is sitting on the porch with Alex reading later that afternoon.

"I knew he would," smiles Alex. "We are pretty funny."

"Maybe we should use the printer and sell funny T-shirts next?" says Jo.

"Hmm... People come in so many shapes and sizes," shrugs Alex.

"We could do a bake sale?" suggests Jo.

"Yes! That's easier. Feeding people is easy. I have yummy recipes from my grandma," responds Alex excitedly, putting down her book.

"Look what I found on my phone. A website with pretty dresses at the mall for the dance," says Jo. "It costs more than what we have made so far, but it's so pretty. What do you think?"

"Wow, that's beautiful. That color would look lovely on you," says Alex. "I left my phone in my room. Can we have a look for one for me?"

"Yes, I already found one I thought you might like. This green one, see?" Jo hands the phone to Alex. "Isn't it pretty?"

Alex thinks the dress is beautiful.

"Well, we have our dresses picked out. Let's get started on baking so we can afford them!" says Alex excitedly.

"If we can save up for bicycles, we can definitely save enough to buy our dresses for the dance!" says Jo.

"Maybe we can make cupcakes and decorate them?" suggests Alex.

"Then we can use our bicycles to ride

to more people, go door to door?" adds Jo.

"As long as you promise not to fall over with them!" teases Alex.

Thank you so much for reading Jo and Alex Summer Adventures!

Please be sure to check out the other books in the series:

Jo and Alex Meet for the First Time
Jo and Alex Down on the Farm
Jo and Alex Best Friends Forever

Your Friend,
L.S. Winters

9 781087 968575